Goodnight, Daniel Tiger

written by Angela C. Santomero

Simon Spotlight

New York   London   Toronto   Sydney   New Delhi

To Hope and Ella.
Everything I do, I do for you!
I'm so proud of you both, and
honored to be your mom!
Ugga Mugga, Mommy

SIMON SPOTLIGHT
An imprint of Simon & Schuster Children's Publishing Division
1230 Avenue of the Americas, New York, New York 10020
First Simon Spotlight paperback edition August 2014
© 2014 The Fred Rogers Company. All rights reserved.
Also available in a Simon Spotlight paper-over-board edition.
All rights reserved, including the right of reproduction in whole or in part in any form.
SIMON SPOTLIGHT and colophon are registered trademarks of Simon & Schuster, Inc.
For information about special discounts for bulk purchases, please contact Simon & Schuster Special Sales
at 1-866-506-1949 or business@simonandschuster.com.
Manufactured in the United States of America 0916 LAK
20 19 18 17 16 15 14 13 12 11
ISBN 978-1-4814-2348-9 (pbk.)
ISBN 978-1-4814-0048-0 (paper over board)
ISBN 978-1-4814-0049-7 (eBook)

This book belongs to:

_____

It was a beautiful day in the neighborhood today, and now it is nighttime. Daniel Tiger needs to get ready for bed! "Ding, ding, ding!" says Daniel, "Tigey wants to go for a trolley ride!"

Daniel wants to play, but . . . it's time to get ready for bed.

"I know you want to play," Mom says as she snuggles with Daniel, "but sleep is important so that you can grow. Do you remember what we do to get ready for bed?"

Daniel smiles and sings with Mom, *"Bathtime, pj's, brush teeth, story and song, and off to bed!"*

"Ding, ding! Hop aboard for a trolley ride to bathtime!"
Dad says.
Daniel laughs and takes a ride. "Ding, ding!"
Daniel wants to play, but . . . it's time to get ready for bed.

Daniel likes bathtime! As he scrubs, he plays and sings, "Scrub, scrub, scrub my fur, up on top my head! Scrubby-scrubby-scrubby-scrub, soon it's time for bed!"

Daniel imagines he is on a boat sailing the soapy seas. He sings, "Sailing, sailing, sailing the soapy seas. Bring all your friends and come with me to sail the soapy seas!"

Daniel wants to play, but . . . it's time to get ready for bed. Dad says, "You need to go to sleep at bedtime so that your great big imagination can rest."

"I do have a lot of imagining I want to do tomorrow!" Daniel says as Dad dries his fur.

Daniel sings, *"Bathtime, pj's, brush teeth, story and song, and off to bed!"* Daniel has taken his bath and now it's time for his favorite trolley pj's.

"Next stop on the trolley ride is brush your teeth," says Dad. Daniel takes his toothbrush and hops up to the sink.

Daniel sings, "I gotta brusha, brusha, brush, brush my teeth at night if I want to keep them healthy and bright. I gotta brusha, brusha, brusha, brush my teeth!" Daniel's teeth are all brushed!

"Let's take Tigey for a ride on Trolley," says Daniel.
"Ding, ding, ding!"
Daniel wants to play, but . . . it's time to get ready for bed.

Mom holds Tigey up to her ear, "Oh, I see," she says to Tigey. Daniel stops playing and looks at Mom. What is she talking about with Tigey?

"Tigey wants to snuggle up in bed and hear a bedtime story," Mom explains.

Daniel climbs up into bed. "Let's read a bedtime story . . . for Tigey," he says. Daniel is getting sleepy.

Daniel snuggles up with Mom as she reads a bedtime story. Reading a story with Mom makes Daniel feel comfy and cozy. Daniel is sleepy. Daniel *does* want to go to bed.

Daniel quietly sings, *"Bathtime, pj's, brush teeth, story and song, and off to bed."* Then he yawns a big tired tiger yawn. Daniel does want to go to bed. Daniel is sleepy.

"Mom and Dad, can you sing me my goodnight song?"

Mom and Dad sing, "Goodnight, Daniel, goodnight. It's time to go to sleep and when you awake, the sun will greet you with its bright and sunny face. Goodnight, Daniel, goodnight." Everyone in the neighborhood is going to sleep too.

Goodnight, Miss Elaina, goodnight.

Goodnight, Prince Wednesday, goodnight.

Goodnight, Katerina Kittycat, goodnight.

Goodnight, O the Owl, goodnight.

Goodnight, Daniel Tiger, goodnight. And goodnight to YOU. Ugga Mugga!